Roxy Hunter and the Secret of the Shaman

By Tracey West

Based on the television movie screenplay
by Robin Dunne and James Kee

PSS!
PRICE STERN SLOAN

PRICE STERN SLOAN
Published by the Penguin Group
Penguin Group (USA) Inc., 375 Hudson Street, New York, New York 10014, USA
Penguin Group (Canada), 90 Eglinton Avenue East, Suite 700, Toronto,
Ontario M4P 2Y3, Canada (a division of Pearson Penguin Canada Inc.)
Penguin Books Ltd., 80 Strand, London WC2R 0RL, England
Penguin Group Ireland, 25 St. Stephen's Green, Dublin 2, Ireland
(a division of Penguin Books Ltd.)
Penguin Group (Australia), 250 Camberwell Road, Camberwell, Victoria 3124, Australia
(a division of Pearson Australia Group Pty. Ltd.)
Penguin Books India Pvt. Ltd., 11 Community Centre, Panchsheel Park,
New Delhi—110 017, India
Penguin Group (NZ), 67 Apollo Drive, Rosedale, North Shore 0632, New Zealand
(a division of Pearson New Zealand Ltd.)
Penguin Books (South Africa) (Pty.) Ltd., 24 Sturdee Avenue,
Rosebank, Johannesburg 2196, South Africa

Penguin Books Ltd., Registered Offices: 80 Strand, London WC2R 0RL, England

Library of Congress Control Number: 2007010519

ISBN 978-0-8431-2665-5   10 9 8 7 6 5 4 3 2 1

Prologue

Eleven-year-old Andy nervously walked across the marsh.

It was late, and only the white moon overhead lit his way. The dark woods ringing the marsh seemed to be closing in on him.

A low wind rustled the tall grasses. It sounded like ghostly whispers.

Then thunder rumbled in the distance, warning of a coming storm.

Andy stopped and listened. *Was* that thunder he had heard? Or was it the roar of some strange . . .

Whoooooooo!

Andy jumped. He looked around, panicked now.

Then an owl flew past him. Andy breathed a sigh of relief.

It's only an owl, he told himself. *Just keep going and you'll be home soon.*

Andy forged ahead.

Creeeeeeeeeak!

He froze again, nearly paralyzed with fear this time. That sound was definitely not an owl.

A new sound crept across the marsh. It came from the woods: the sound of twigs snapping.

Someone was coming.

"H-h-hello?" Andy called out nervously. He was beginning to regret taking the shortcut. Every kid in Serenity Falls knew the Legend of the Black Marsh Monster. People had been claiming they'd heard strange sounds and seen a monstrous figure in the marsh for years. But Andy had never believed it—at least not until tonight.

"Anybody there?" he called out, his voice croaking.

But nobody answered.

It's just your imagination, Andy told himself. *Just your imagination. Just your imagination . . .*

He repeated the chant and walked on.

Then a huge, hulking figure ran out of the woods. The monstrous, hunched form blocked the path ahead.

"*Aaaaaaaaaaaaah!*" Andy screamed louder than

he had ever screamed in his life. He turned and ran back down the trail.

Andy took the long way home that night.

Chapter One:
· · · The Monster of the Black Marsh · · ·

Roxy Hunter sat with her legs crossed on the library floor. For once, she was excited to be at Serenity Falls Day Camp.

Sure, she didn't mind the idea of going to the town library every day. But what made camp unbearable was the camp director, Ms. Slausen. She was Roxy's nemesis. They had been mortal enemies ever since Roxy decided to feed the fish in the fish tank. (How could Slausen possibly *know* that fish don't eat bananas? They seemed to like them just fine to Roxy.) Not only was Slausen always yelling at Roxy, but she always made the kids do activities with stuff like Popsicle sticks and glue—total baby stuff. Roxy would rather have spent her time at the camp exploring the library shelves. But Ms. Slausen was so strict, she insisted on keeping everyone together all of the time.

Today, however, was different. Today Roxy's favorite author, Lorne Red Deer, was there. He was reading from his novel *Tanaka the Orphan Warrior: Curse of the Caribou Ghost.*

Roxy listened, dreamy eyed, as Lorne told the story in his deep voice.

"But Tanaka could see by her eyes that her place was here, with her grandmother. The curse had been lifted, and the spirits had been appeased," Lorne read.

Then another voice hissed over Lorne's. Seth was whispering to his two friends, Timmy and Tommy.

"Andy was cutting through the marsh so he wouldn't get caught in the rain," Seth whispered loudly. "Instead, he got caught by the Monster of the Black Marsh."

"No way!" Tommy said.

"What did it look like?" asked Timmy, his twin brother.

"It was covered in roots and moss and green, slimy pond scum, and salamanders crawled out of its black, dead eyes," Seth said.

Tommy looked doubtful. "That's baloney!"

But Seth leaned in closer, a knowing look

in his eyes. "Why do you think Andy's not here today?"

Roxy couldn't take it anymore. She turned to face the boys.

"Will you three chowderheads be quiet, puh-leaze!" she said, annoyed.

"Why don't you be quiet?" Tommy shot back.

"Yeah, Hoxy Runter," said Timmy.

Roxy wasn't fazed. "So sad," she said, shaking her head. "Two brothers born with only one brain."

Seth scowled. "What's your problem?" he asked.

"My problem is your lack of culture," Roxy sniffed. "I consider Mr. Red Deer the Joyce James of children's literature, and your constant nattering—"

"Ms. Hunter!"

Roxy looked up. Lorne Red Deer had stopped reading his book. Ms. Slausen was standing over her, a frown on her pinched face. Her eyes looked angry behind her thick glasses.

That was typical, Roxy thought. The boys are rude and she gets in trouble. She started to protest. "But Ms. Slausen, I was *simply* trying to—"

"You will *simply* sit and listen quietly,

otherwise you will be asked to leave," Ms. Slausen snapped. "Again!"

Roxy knew arguing with Ms. Slausen was no use. She turned and gave a little bow to Lorne Red Deer. She had worn silver feather earrings for the occasion, and they shone against her blond hair.

"You have my sincerest apology, oh great and mighty writer," Roxy said solemnly.

"Uh, no problem," Lorne replied, trying not to laugh. He had never met a fan quite like Roxy before. He picked up his book again and began to read. "And so, once more, with only his trusted wolf, Swiftfoot, at his side, Tanaka walked toward the horizon as the sinking sun brushed the sky with fire. The end."

The day-camp kids all clapped. Roxy jumped to her feet.

"Bravo! Bravo! Author! Author!" she cried enthusiastically.

Ms. Slausen instructed the campers to line up so they could meet Lorne and get their books autographed. Most kids had one book, but Roxy had an armful.

"Don't forget to tell your parents to visit my Web site and click on Tanaka's tepee to view the full line of Tanaka merchandise," Lorne was saying.

"This month, when you buy three books, you get a free Tanaka key chain."

Roxy walked up to the table and plopped her books in front of Lorne. The author looked a little surprised.

"Mr. Red Deer, I'm Roxy Hunter," she said. "I just want to say what an honor it is to meet you."

Lorne grabbed the top book off the stack and began to sign.

"Roxy Hunter? That sounds familiar," he said.

"Well, I have written you on the odd occasion," Roxy said conspiratorially. "Twelve odd occasions, to be exact. In my last letter, I outlined a new character I felt the Tanaka series needs."

Lorne raised an eyebrow. "Oh, *that* Roxy Hunter."

"Her name is Princess Roxahana," Roxy said. "An Iroquois warrioress and near orphan. Anyway, I'd love to describe it in greater detail. But before we do . . ."

Roxy took a piece of paper from a pocket in her shorts. "Would you mind signing here, here, and here?" she asked, pointing to different spots on the paper.

"What is this?" Lorne asked.

Roxy smiled. "Just a friendly little nondisposure contract."

Lorne looked stunned. "Excuse me? A *nondisclosure* contract?" he asked.

"You know—a legal thingy guaranteeing my rights in perpetuosity. You know those pesky lawyers: heaven forbid Princess Roxahana show up in your next book without my name on the cover."

"Your rights in *perpetuity?* Okaaaaay," Lorne said slowly. He couldn't believe she was serious!

Yes, Roxy was definitely not like any fan he had ever met.

Or *anyone* he had ever met, for that matter!

10

Chapter Two:
• • • Swiftfoot • • •

Roxy skipped through the green fields surrounding her house. The late summer sun shone down, warming her skin.

She was free! Free of Ms. Slausen, free of the dusty library shelves . . . free to let her imagination roam.

Right now she was no longer Roxy Hunter, a nine-and-a-half-year-old girl, originally from New Jersey, now a resident of Serenity Falls. No. She was Princess Roxahana, Iroquois warrioress.

Roxy staggered through the tall grass of the field.

"And so, her life fading quickly, her wounds too much to bear, Princess Roxahana struggles on," Roxy said, her voice choking dramatically. "Must warn village. Got to . . . save . . . them . . ."

Roxy collapsed.

"Unable to take another step, Princess Roxahana's last hope lies with . . ."

Roxy stopped. Something was coming toward her—something real, not imaginary. It looked like a dog.

"Swiftfoot?" Roxy asked. Swiftfoot was the wolf sidekick from Lorne Red Deer's stories, and if she was to be Princess Roxahana, then she would need her very own Swiftfoot. This dog would fill the bill perfectly!

The big, scruffy dog ran up to Roxy and began to lick her face. Roxy laughed and sat up. Swiftfoot rolled onto his back, and Roxy rubbed his belly.

"Aren't you a handsome fellow?" Roxy asked.

Swiftfoot barked in agreement. Roxy scratched the dog's neck. She noticed that he had no collar.

"Don't you have an owner?" she asked.

Swiftfoot got to his feet and gave Roxy another lick.

"Well, this is great, because I don't have a dog!" Roxy cried. "Do you want to be my sidekick?"

"*Woof!*" Swiftfoot barked.

"Great!" Roxy said; then her smile faded.

"We've just got to work on Mom. That's going to be tricky."

Then a sound rang through the field—the sound of a dinner bell.

"Roxy! Dinnertime!" Roxy's mom called out.

"Aw, flibbersnibbets, that's Mom," Roxy said, frowning. She looked into Swiftfoot's brown eyes. "Here's the plan. You stay here, and I'll come back later with some dinner for you. Would you like that?"

Swiftfoot wagged his tail happily.

"All right," Roxy said, satisfied. "You stay here. I'll be back."

Swiftfoot watched as Roxy ran away.

Roxy ran toward the Moody Mansion, the old, stone house she lived in with her mom and best friend, Max. The Moody Mansion was a maze of rooms and towers. As Roxy headed inside, her mom, Susan, got dinner ready in the kitchen with the help of her boyfriend, Jon.

"I'll pick up the confetti on my way back from the city tomorrow," Jon was saying.

"I've lived here only a few months," Susan said teasingly. "How did you manage to rope me into this?"

Jon playfully hugged her. "It must have been

my raw charisma," he said teasingly.

Susan laughed, and Roxy walked through the kitchen door.

"Hey, Jon," Roxy said. "Hey, Mom. Can I have a dog?"

Susan sighed. It seemed that lately Roxy asked that question a hundred times a day.

"I've told you, dear, we'll see," Susan said patiently.

"Is that 'we' as in you and I, or 'we' as in you?" Roxy asked.

"'We' as in me," Susan said firmly.

"I thought we lived in a democracy!" Roxy argued.

Jon smiled. "Not until you're old enough to vote."

"Roxy, will you please tell Max dinner is ready?" Susan asked. "He's in the study."

Roxy bowed deeply. "Yes, Your Highness!"

Roxy walked through the house to the study, debating whether to tell Max about Swiftfoot. Even though Max was three years older than she, and some kind of supergenius to boot, he was her best friend in the whole world. Max lived with Roxy and her mom while his archaeologist parents traveled around the world. Roxy knew Max missed his parents, but she was glad he was around.

Roxy opened the door to the study to find Max sitting at the desk next to a pretty, blond teenage girl. The girl was holding Max's eyeglasses, and Max's face was bright red.

"Oh, you look so cute without your glasses on!" the girl was saying.

"Am I interrupting?" Roxy asked suspiciously.

"Um, no," Max said. He quickly put on his glasses. "Roxy, this is Jill. Jill, this is Roxy. She's . . ."

"His fiancée," Roxy said quickly, narrowing her eyes at Jill.

"His fiancée?" Jill squealed. "That is sooo cute!"

"Isn't it just," Roxy said. Her voice was ice cold. Max was *her* friend—she was not okay with Jill hanging around. She turned to Max. "Max, dear, we're requested at the dinner table."

Then Roxy looked at Jill. "If we all eat a little less, I'm sure there would be enough for you," she said, her voice dripping with sarcastic sweetness.

"No, thanks," Jill said brightly, oblivious to Roxy's mounting jealousy.

15

A car horn beeped outside.

"That's my ride!" Jill said. She grabbed a backpack hanging over her chair. She stuffed some books inside.

"Thanks again, Maxie," she said. "Nice meeting you, Roxy!"

Then she ran out.

Roxy turned to Max, an eyebrow raised. "Maxie?"

Max didn't respond. He followed Roxy to the dining room, where they joined Susan and Jon at the dinner table. Susan passed around plates of delicious food.

"So, how's the French tutoring going?" Susan asked Max.

"Yes, French, the language of *love*," Roxy said, shooting daggers at Max with her eyes.

Susan and Jon giggled. Max blushed.

"It's fine," Max mumbled, focusing intently on his plate.

Roxy looked over at Jon, and they shared a smile. She had been pretty upset when her mom had started dating him. She didn't want anyone to take her dad's place. But Jon made her mom happy. And he was really nice, too.

Jon turned to Susan. "I almost forgot.

Tomorrow morning, we've got to go take a look at the crystal centerpiece. They want to do the unveiling before the dance."

"So what is a sesquisemteminal, anyway?" Roxy asked.

"*Sesquicentennial*," Susan corrected her.

"It's the 150th anniversary of Serenity Falls," Jon explained.

"Hmm. Sesquicentennial. Is that *French*, Max?" Roxy teased. Her eyes sparkled.

Max blushed. "Latin, actually," he said.

"I wonder if poor Jill could even spell that?" Roxy asked innocently.

Susan shook her head. "Roxy, no teasing," she warned. "So, who wants more beet salad?"

Roxy and Max were silent.

"Uh, sure, I'll have some more," Jon offered.

Roxy turned to her mom. "Boy, he must really like you," she said.

"What?" Susan asked.

"Mom, no one believes in the importance of a healthy and balanced meal for a growing child more than I," she said. She frowned at the beet salad. "But there are limits."

"Beets are healthful," Susan said.

"Not the way you do them," Roxy muttered.

"Well, *I* like the way she does them," Jon said.

Roxy shook her head. "You're just like Dad."

Susan looked startled. "What do you mean?"

"Dad used to lie about the beet salad as well," Roxy said. "But he would hide it in his napkin."

Max and Jon laughed, but Susan was quiet. Then the doorbell rang.

"I'll get it! *Excusez-moi!*" Roxy said as she walked past Max.

Roxy opened the door to find a large man in a sheriff's uniform standing there. He chomped on a strange-looking yellow candy bar.

Roxy stared at the man for a moment.

"Ma! It's the law!" she yelled. "Should I ask to see a warrant?"

"Roxy!" Susan scolded as she walked up behind Roxy. Roxy shrugged and led the officer inside. She recognized him from town—his name was Martin Potts.

"Evening, all," said Potts. "Sorry to interrupt, but I'm going door-to-door to warn folks to be on the lookout for anything suspicious."

"What kind of suspicious?" Susan asked.

"I'm afraid it's rather serious. There have been some robberies in the last few days," Potts explained gravely. "Some people have reported that garbage has gone missing."

"Those darn garbagemen—taking the garbage again," Jon joked, giving Roxy a wink.

Potts scowled at Jon but otherwise ignored the joke. "Also, the stone eagle was stolen from the top of the library, and several flags have gone missing from government buildings," he went on. "Since you and Susan are on the decorations committee, I thought I'd put you on alert."

"You think some kids are going to steal our banners?" Jon asked.

"These could be dangerous criminals. If you do see anything, please call us—don't try to handle a volatile situation like that yourself. We know how to handle thieves properly," Potts said seriously. He scanned the dinner table. "Is that beet salad?"

"Um, yes," Susan said, trying not to giggle. "Would you like some?"

"I'm sure he would," Jon cut in quickly. "But he'd better keep warning the other neighbors."

"You're right," Potts said, and nodded. He tipped his hat to Susan. "Duty calls, ma'am. Just remember—stay on watch!"

Jon ushered the officer toward the door.

"Will do, Bull. Thanks for the warning."

Potts tapped his badge smugly. "It's *Sheriff Potts*, Jon. Not Bull."

"Your badge says '*Deputy* Sheriff,'" Roxy pointed out.

Potts's face turned red. He awkwardly checked his watch.

"Gotta go," he said. "Stay alert!"

Roxy closed the door behind the deputy sheriff as she thought about what he'd said.

Was there another mystery to solve in Serenity Falls? That could be interesting. A few months before, someone tried to steal the land around the Moody Mansion. Luckily, Roxy and Max had solved that case.

"Do you think we should be worried?" Susan asked, peering out the window.

"Nah, Bull's only acting like it's a big deal so he can sound important. I'm sure it's just some kids playing pranks—besides, who's going to miss stolen garbage?" Jon answered, chuckling to himself.

Roxy walked slowly back to the dinner table. Jon was probably right. The thefts didn't sound like a big deal.

Still, if a mystery needed solving, she'd be ready for it . . .

Chapter Three:
• • • Into the Woods • • •

After dinner, Jon and Susan cleared the
table. Jon talked excitedly about plans for the
town's celebration, but Susan was strangely quiet.

"Are you okay?" Jon asked.

"Oh, yeah," Susan said absently. "I'm just a
little concerned about what Deputy Potts said."

"I wouldn't worry about it," Jon replied. "Bull
has a tendency to be overly dramatic."

"Why do you call him Bull?" Susan asked.

"Well, back in high school, Martin wasn't
all that popular," Jon said. "Our school mascot
was a bull, so Martin thought he would look cool
riding the school mascot into one of the dances.
Unfortunately, he picked the wrong dance—
Valentine's Day!"

"Why?" Susan cried. "What happened?"

"All those red decorations made the bull crazy," Jon said. "The gym had to be evacuated. Luckily, nobody was hurt, but since then, everyone's called him Bull."

Susan laughed a little, but she felt bad for Deputy Sheriff Potts. "That's mean."

"You think?" Jon asked.

Susan raised one eyebrow questioningly.

"Nah. It's just a harmless nickname," he continued, shaking his head.

Roxy entered the dining room, carrying a basket of laundry.

"Dishes are done," Roxy announced.

Susan looked at the basket, confused. "What's that, hon?"

"Thought I'd put away the laundry and then hit the hay," Roxy replied.

"It's not your bedtime," Susan said, even more puzzled.

"It is somewhere in the world," Roxy pointed out. "Anyway, big day at day camp tomorrow. I think we're making macaroni art. Gotta be sharp."

She gave her mom a kiss on the cheek.

"Good night, Mom," she said.

"Good night, dear," Susan replied.

Then Roxy walked over to Jon and kissed

him on the cheek. "Good night, Jon."

"Night, Roxstar," Jon said, smiling.

Roxy left the room and carried the basket upstairs. She passed Max's bedroom, then stopped.

Max's door was open. He stood in front of his mirror, taking his glasses on and off.

"What are you doing?" Roxy asked.

Max jumped, surprised. "Nothing," he said quickly.

Roxy shrugged. "Okay. Good night . . . *monsieur*!"

Roxy took the laundry basket to her room and shut the door behind her.

The clean dishes, the laundry, the early bedtime—it was all part of a plan, of course. Roxy took the clothes off the top of the laundry basket. Underneath was a package of rice cakes, some leftover chicken, and an apple. She stuffed them into her knapsack.

Then she took a flashlight and batteries out of the basket and put those in her knapsack, too.

Finally, she took the clothes and shoved them under the top blanket on her bed. She squished and shaped them until they looked like a Roxy-size, sleeping, nine-and-a-half-year-old girl.

Roxy grinned, satisfied. She slung the

knapsack over her shoulder. Then she opened her window and climbed out.

Roxy carefully made her way down the wooden trellis attached to the side of the house. When she was just a few feet above the ground, she jumped. It wasn't the first time she had made a sneaky escape from her bedroom.

Roxy cautiously looked from side to side. The coast was clear. She ran into the dark night, toward the field.

When Roxy reached the field, she took the chicken out of her pack.

"Swiftfoot," she called softly. "Here, boy!"

There was no response. Roxy tried again, a little louder this time.

"Got some food for you," she coaxed, whistling quietly.

As her eyes adjusted to the darkness, she saw a shape emerge from the woods that ringed the Moody Mansion. The shape looked like the dog, but Roxy wasn't completely sure.

"Swiftfoot?" she asked.

The shape turned and melted back into the forest. Roxy nervously bit her lip. She hadn't counted on that.

But she had promised Swiftfoot she would

come back. Roxy took a deep breath. She took the flashlight from her pack and turned it on.

Then she walked into the woods.

Swiftfoot—if it was the dog—had gone down a crude path.

As Roxy shone the flashlight ahead, she saw trees, bushes, and not much else.

Then she heard a sound—the sound of something or someone heading toward her. She froze.

Swiftfoot ran out of the brush! He came over to Roxy, his tail wagging.

Roxy gave him the chicken, and he hungrily ate it.

"Look, I've got more food for you," she told the dog. "Mom's going to take a little more convincing, so you'll have to stay in the garage for now. Come on."

Roxy took a few steps, but Swiftfoot didn't budge.

"Don't worry. It's five stars as far as garages go," Roxy assured him.

Swiftfoot turned around. He headed down the path—deeper into the woods!

"Hey! Where are you going!" she called out.

Roxy frowned. She was far enough from

25

home already. But curiosity got the best of her. She followed the dog.

As she continued on, the trees thinned out a bit. Roxy wasn't familiar with this part of the woods. She paused and shone her flashlight around.

She gasped. To her right, the edge of the trail descended into a deep ravine. The rocky slope led to a streambed about twenty feet below.

Roxy went more slowly now, careful not to fall over the side. Then she heard a sound—a sound like the tinkling of broken glass.

"Swiftfoot?" Roxy called softly. She pressed on.

Then she heard another sound. The sound of footsteps crunching on fallen twigs. But these weren't the pitter-patter of doggy feet. They were much louder and heavier.

"The Marsh Monster," Roxy whispered, remembering Seth's story. Cold fear crept throughout her body.

Then a dark shadow crossed the path in front of her.

"Ahhhh!" Roxy screamed.

She turned and began to run, but her foot slipped on the crumbling trail. She lost her balance. Then she fell . . .

She tumbled down the hill, desperately grabbing for something to hold on to. There was nothing. She dug her sneakers into the rocky dirt, slowing herself down a bit.

With a quiet thud, she landed at the bottom of the hill. She was scared, but not hurt. She looked up.

The Marsh Monster towered over her!

"*Aaaaah!* Please don't eat me!" Roxy screamed, covering her eyes with her hands.

But nothing happened. The Marsh Monster didn't move, and Roxy finally was brave enough to sneak a peek through her fingers. The figure standing over her was a man. He was dirty and disheveled, with wild hair and a beard, but he was definitely a man, not a monster.

"Okay?" the man asked.

"What?" Roxy replied, dropping her hands.

"You. Okay?" he asked again.

Roxy paused. The man's eyes were gentle and kind.

"I guess," she said.

"Good," said the man. "Good girl. Go home. Woods not safe."

Roxy wasn't sure what to make of him. "What?"

"Good girl. Go home to family. Safe," said the man.

The ragged man picked up an old sack and slung it over his shoulder. It jingled and clanked as it moved. Then he turned and walked back along the path.

Suddenly, Swiftfoot ran up and walked at the man's heels. The man and dog walked off together.

"Is Swiftfoot your dog?" Roxy asked. She jumped to her feet. "Hey! Wait a second!"

Chapter Four:
• • • The Shaman • • •

Roxy chased after the man. She caught up to him in a small clearing in the middle of the woods. A fire burned near a tent fashioned together from old poles, blankets, and plastic tarps.

"Hey, mister. Do you live here?" Roxy asked.

"You should go home," the man said. He put the sack down on the ground and began to take things from it. It looked like a bunch of garbage to Roxy: an old hubcap, glass bottles, and a broken lamp.

"What's all this? Are you some kind of collector or something?" Roxy asked.

But the man didn't seem to be paying attention to Roxy. He mumbled to himself as he pulled more items from the bag.

"Preparations . . . not much time . . . not much time . . . have to be ready . . . have to be ready."

Roxy scanned the camp. Behind the tent was a strange-looking machine of some kind. It seemed to be made of an old bicycle, metal pipes, car batteries, and a bunch of other stuff. The machine pointed at a platform that sat tall on wooden legs. Broken mirrors surrounded the platform.

Curious, Roxy walked over. She touched the strange machine.

"No touch! Delicate!" the man cried with alarm in his voice.

Roxy backed off. "Good girl," he said. Then he continued muttering. "Calibration . . . occipital refraction . . . delicate."

"What's it do?" Roxy asked.

The man looked at Roxy, as though deciding whether to trust her. Then he bent down and picked up a broken tree branch. He dipped the end of the dried, brown branch into the fire. Then he held it up, like a torch.

Stars appeared in the surrounding trees, twinkling with flaming light. Roxy gasped. How could that be?

Then, as her eyes adjusted to the light, she saw that tiny mirrors dangled from the tree branches all around her. There were mirrors, glass, and bits of metal, all reflecting the light from the torch.

"It's magic!" Roxy said with awe in her voice.

The man turned to her. His face beamed with pride and happiness.

"Yes! Magic!" he cried. "She will come from the sky."

"Who will?" Roxy asked.

The man pointed at Roxy. "Like you. Like you. From the sky."

He continued sorting through his pile of junk. Roxy was confused.

"Like me? But I'm from Jersey," she told him.

"It's late," the man said. "You should go."

Roxy looked at her watch. "Yipes! You're right."

She clicked on her flashlight. "Can I come back tomorrow and play with your dog?" she asked.

"Dog?" the man replied. He looked over at Swiftfoot. "Not my dog. Comes and goes. Stray."

Roxy smiled. "Great! See you tomorrow!"

Roxy climbed back up the ravine, found the trail, and headed home as fast as she could. She climbed into the house through her bedroom window. The fake Roxy was still there, under the covers.

Roxy was tired, but there was something she had to find out. Seeing the man had reminded her of something—something in one of Lorne Red Deer's books. She ran to her bookshelf. She scooped up every Tanaka book she had and then dumped them onto her bed.

Using the flashlight, Roxy shuffled through them until she found what she was looking for. She held up a book titled *Tanaka and the Shaman's Treasure*.

Roxy flipped through the pages. Finally she found the right page and began to read out loud.

"Then he thrust the flaming branch to the ground. Like magic, the ceiling burst into light, as though the shaman had brought the night sky down and captured it in the cave," she read.

Her mind raced. That was exactly what she had just witnessed in the woods! She put down the book.

"Wow," Roxy whispered. "The man in the woods is a shaman!"

She picked up the book and continued reading eagerly: "Shamen were Native American mystics, and they always had apprentices—young people who helped the shaman perform rites and rituals." Roxy smiled to herself. She was a young person and her shaman was apprentice-less—so logically, she should be this shaman's apprentice!

Chapter Five:

• • • Lemon Boofoo • • •

The next morning, Roxy went with her mom and Jon to the town hall to do some planning for the sesquicentennial. They needed the help of the town's acting mayor, Saul Bloomberg.

Roxy watched as Mayor Bloomberg paced around his office. He was short and sweaty, and really nervous, Roxy thought. But the last mayor, Peter Middleton, had kidnapped Max and tried to steal the Moody Mansion. So this one was definitely an improvement.

"I woke up this morning, and my glands were swollen," Bloomberg said, sounding panicked. "Swollen to the size of golf balls! Why do I have to make the speech? I don't know how to make speeches. I'm an accountant!"

"Well, you're the mayor, Saul," Jon pointed out.

"*Acting* mayor, Jon," Bloomberg said. "Acting mayor. I was only supposed to take the job until they found someone new. Why haven't they found someone new?"

"The wheels of democracy turn slowly, Mr. Bloomberg," Roxy said solemnly.

"Who are you, Thomas Jefferson?" Bloomberg snapped.

Someone knocked on the door, and the mayor jumped. The door opened and Deputy Sheriff Potts walked in, carrying an architect's tube and a box.

"Sorry I'm late," he said. "I had some urgent police business to attend to."

He walked over to the mayor's desk and put down the box. Then he took a set of blueprints from the tube.

"I don't think I have to tell you that anything you see here doesn't leave this room," Potts said. "What I am about to show you are the plans for the Serenity Falls monument that is going to be unveiled at the sesquicentennial. It's like nothing you've ever seen before."

He unrolled the blueprints.

"It's a lighthouse," Susan said flatly.

"A five-foot-tall lighthouse," Jon added just as flatly.

"Yes!" Potts said. His face was flush with excitement. "The lighthouse will be the centerpiece, donated at great expense by my family."

Potts opened the box and pulled out a large crystal lens. "This lens will go inside the lighthouse to create the beam of light coming from its tower."

"I thought that a lighthouse was something that warns people away," Roxy said.

Jon tried not to laugh.

"A lighthouse is a symbol of light," Potts explained patiently. "A beacon of freedom. A call to shelter and peace." He pointed to the old safe in the office. "If you'd be so kind, Mr. Mayor, I think the crystal should be locked in the safe."

"Of course," Bloomberg replied.

Someone knocked on the door again, and this time, Sheriff Tom Dawson walked in.

"Sorry to interrupt, Mr. Mayor," he said.

"*Acting* mayor!" Bloomberg cried.

Sheriff Tom looked around the room. "Well hello, Susan, Jon," he said. Then he spied Roxy and smiled. "Roxy! How's my favorite little detective today?"

"Fine, thank you, Sheriff Tom," Roxy said.

"Glad to hear it," the sheriff replied. "Listen, Bull, that darn cat you rescued this morning ran back up that tree. You better have a look-see."

Potts nodded. "Uh, yeah. I'll get right on it."

Sheriff Tom tipped his hat. "See you, folks."

Then the two officers left, shutting the door behind them.

Roxy looked at Jon. "Urgent police business?"

Jon laughed. He looked at Susan, but she wouldn't meet his eyes. Instead, she turned to Roxy.

"Let's get you to day camp, honey," she said.

* * * ♥ * * *

While Roxy got ready for a day of macaroni art, Max sat in Lenny's Coffee Shop. He wasn't wearing his glasses, and getting dressed that morning, he had put his T-shirt over a long-sleeved shirt. He had seen some high-school boys dressed like that once, and they looked pretty cool.

His friend Ramma walked over to the table, wearing an apron. Ramma was a medical student from India who had camped out in the attic of the

38

Moody Mansion before Roxy, Susan, and Max moved in. Now he lived with Jon and worked in the coffee shop when he wasn't at school.

"Dude, you are looking very stylish," he told Max. "Perhaps somebody is trying to make an impression on a certain somebody else?"

"Who? Jill?" Max shrugged, trying to act casual, but his voice was cracking a little. "I'm just tutoring her for summer school, Ramma. Besides, she's fifteen, and I'm twelve."

Ramma leaned over the table. "I tell you, if you want to look a little more mature, I've got just the thing."

He reached into his back pocket and pulled out a candy bar wrapped in yellow paper. He handed it to Max.

"Lemon Boofoo," Ramma announced. "All the sophisticated dudes are eating them back home."

Max looked at it. There was unfamiliar writing on the wrapper.

"Lemon Boofoo? What's in it?" Max asked.

"Lemon, yogurt, and kombucha," Ramma replied.

Max was still puzzled. "Kombucha?"

"It is a kind of fungus—like a mushroom," Ramma explained.

Max grimaced. "I think I'll pass."

He handed the candy bar back to Ramma.

"My uncle is trying to introduce them to America," Ramma said, frowning. "Ever since he found out I got this job here, he keeps sending me them from home. But not for my life can I get people to try them. The only person who eats them is that Deputy Sheriff Potts. And I am thinking he is not such an effective endorsement."

The coffee shop door opened, and Jill bounced in.

"Hey, Max! Sorry I'm late," she said.

Ramma gave Max a knowing wink and walked away. Jill slid into the seat across from Max.

"Hey, Jill," Max said. "I thought we'd start on the passé composé today. That's the 'compound past tense,' from chapter eleven."

"Um, about that," Jill said. "Listen, the gang is getting together for a barbecue down by the river today, and I was wondering . . ."

Max got a lump in his throat. "Yeah?" he asked, hoping she might invite him.

"Um, well, would you mind doing my homework for me?" Jill asked, her voice as sweet as sugar. "I'll totally look it over later, it's just . . . you know."

Max tried not to act disappointed. That wouldn't be cool.

"Oh. Sure," Max said.

Jill smiled, and Max forgot all about being disappointed. "Thanks, Max. You're the best!"

She plopped her book on the table in front of Max, then stood up.

"Is that a new shirt?" she asked. "Wow. You little cutie."

Jill walked out the door, stopping to wave at Max.

"See you later!" she called out.

Ramma walked over to the table, grinning at Max.

"Want a milk shake, cutie?" he teased.

Chapter Six:
• • • The Search for a Legend • • •

Roxy had managed to sneak away from the rest of the day campers, and now she sat at a library table, surrounded by a stack of books.

She closed the book she was reading in frustration.

"Can't find it!" she fumed.

A tall, thin man in a dark suit appeared next to Roxy.

"Ms. Hunter, shouldn't you be with the other children?" he asked.

Roxy looked up to see Mr. Tibers, the librarian. "Not if I can help it," she answered.

Mr. Tibers was one of Roxy's favorite people in Serenity Falls. Not only was he the keeper of the library and a fountain of knowledge, but he loved a good mystery almost as much as she did!

Roxy knew that if anyone would help her, it would be him.

"Do you have Ms. Slausen's permission to be in the reference section?" Mr. Tibers asked patiently.

"Sauerkraut? Of course not. She hates me," Roxy replied. Then she lowered her voice to a whisper. "Besides, there's a mystery to solve."

The librarian raised an eyebrow. "A mystery, you say?"

"I'm looking for a native legend. Something about a girl from the sky. Or a girl from New Jersey. I'm not sure," Roxy explained.

Like any good librarian, Mr. Tibers was intrigued by the challenge.

"Well, shall we narrow the search?" he asked. His normally pale face colored just slightly with excitement. "Navajo, Sioux, Cree? Remember, native cultures and languages are extraordinarily diverse."

Roxy thought for a moment. "I guess it would be from around here," she said finally.

"Ah, that would be the Iroquois nation," Mr. Tibers said.

"Iroquois, yeah!" Roxy exclaimed. It made sense. "Just like Tanaka."

"It's a shame you didn't ask my good friend Lorne Red Deer while he was here yesterday," the librarian said. "He is well versed in Iroquois mythology."

Roxy jumped up from her seat. "Of course! What's his number?"

"Pardon?" Mr. Tibers grew nervous. Lorne loved his fans. But getting a call at home from a fan—especially a fan like Roxy . . .

"Give me his number," Roxy said. "I'll call him now."

"I can't just give out his telephone number," Mr. Tibers sputtered.

"Why?" Roxy asked. "This is really important, Mr. Tibers. He won't mind. He and I are practically in business together."

Mr. Tibers shook his head. "I'm sorry, no."

"Pleeeeeeeease?" Roxy asked.

"No," Mr. Tibers said firmly.

"Pleeeeeeeeeeeeeeeeeease?" Roxy asked.

"No, Ms. Hunter," Mr. Tibers said.

But Roxy wouldn't give up.

"Pleeeeeeeeeeeeeeeeeeeeeeeeeeeeease?"

"Fine!" the librarian huffed.

Moments later, Roxy was dialing Lorne Red Deer's number from a pay phone outside the library. The author was home, practicing his golf swing in his rec room. Then his phone rang.

"Yel-lo," Lorne answered.

"Mr. Red Deer? This is Roxy Hunter," Roxy began. "Remember? From yesterday? I gave you the Princess Roxahana outline."

"Oh. Riiiight," Lorne said slowly as he realized who was calling.

"Have you had a chance to look it over yet?" Roxy asked.

"No, not yet," Lorne said, annoyed. "I've been crazy busy."

"No problem. I'm sure you'll get around to it," Roxy hurried on. "Anyway, the reason I'm calling you is I need some information on a shaman ceremony involving lights in the sky and a little girl. Possibly from New Jersey."

"Well, let's see," Lorne replied. "There's the one about the girl from the northern lights . . ."

"Girl from the northern lights! That must be it!" Roxy cried, interrupting him. "What's the ceremony for that?"

"I'm not sure if there is one." Lorne thought for a moment. "Wait. How did you even get this number?"

Roxy was about to answer when she suddenly

had that feeling that someone was watching her. She looked up to see the pinched face of Ms. Slausen glaring at her. She had to cover, quick.

"Okay, Mom, I'll make sure to pick up the milk," Roxy said into the phone. "Love you, too."

She quickly hung up the phone and tried to give Ms. Slausen her most cheerful smile.

On the other end of the line, Lorne Red Deer stared at the phone, puzzled.

Mom? he wondered.

Chapter Seven:
• • • The Marsh Monster Returns • • •

Down the street from the library, Susan and Jon worked together at the local bank. But even though Jon was wearing a neatly pressed business suit, he wasn't exactly working very hard.

"Nash, at the buzzer," he said. He held a ball of crumpled paper in one hand, and he tossed it at a wastebasket across the room. The paper hit its mark. "And it's good for three!"

Susan walked by his desk.

"Hey there, pretty bank-worker-lady-type person," he said cheerfully.

"Hi," Susan said, in a voice that wasn't quite as cheerful. "Did you get the confetti?"

"Yes, I'ma buy you the best confetti money can a buy," Jon replied in a silly accent. He picked up a big bag from the floor and put it on his desk. Susan looked inside the bag and scowled.

"Jon, this confetti is pink," she said, her normally cheerful brown eyes looking tired. "You were supposed to get red, white, and blue."

"Well, technically pink is red and white mixed together . . ." Jon joked. But Susan didn't seem to think it was funny.

"Fine," she said.

"Susan, this was the only confetti they had left. No one will notice," he said. He looked at her with concern. She wasn't acting like the Susan he had come to know. "Are you okay?"

"I'm just a little overwhelmed, that's all," she replied, brushing a strand of shoulder-length dark hair from her face. "It's nothing."

Jon nodded. "Okay. Are we still on for *Casablanca* tonight?"

Susan hesitated. "Actually, I haven't been spending enough mother-daughter time with Roxy," she said. "I thought I'd stay in tonight. Do you mind?"

"Oh, no, not at all," Jon said. "That's a good idea. I totally understand. No problem."

"Great. Thanks," Susan said. She gave Jon a weak smile. "I'd better get back to work."

The end of day camp that day came with a few hours of freedom for Roxy. She used it to pack up some more food for Swiftfoot and the shaman. Then she headed off toward the woods.

As soon as she set foot on the trail, Swiftfoot came bounding toward her. He leaped up and licked her face.

Roxy laughed and patted his head. She held out the paper bag she carried in her hand.

"Look! I brought you guys some food. Do you like cheese?" she asked. She took out a block of cheese and fed some to the dog. "I was going to bring you some animal crackers, but I figured it was too much like cannibalism."

Swiftfoot gratefully wagged his tail. Then Roxy heard something behind her—it was the sound of voices, coming from the field.

Through the trees, she could see Seth, Andy, Timmy, and Tommy walking toward them, along with a few other boys. They all carried baseball bats or hockey sticks.

"Oh no!" Roxy cried. The boys were probably coming after the Marsh Monster. But instead, they would find the shaman. That wouldn't be good.

She turned to Swiftfoot. "We can't let them find you and the shaman," she said. She held out the paper bag. "Take this food and go. I'll think of something."

Swiftfoot bit down on the bag.

"Go!" Roxy said urgently.

Swiftfoot ran off, carrying the bag in his mouth. The dog was safe for now. But Roxy had to keep the boys away—for good.

"Think, Roxy, think," she muttered to herself.

She saw the boys stop right in front of the trail. Andy, the boy who had seen the Marsh Monster, looked very pale.

"I can't go back in there," he said.

Seth held up his baseball bat. "Don't worry, man. If there really is a monster in there, he better start saying his prayers," he said boldly.

Suddenly Roxy broke from the trees, screaming loudly.

"*Aaaaaaaaaaaaaaaah!*"

She ran right into the boys and threw her arms around Seth.

"Oh, it was horrible!" she cried dramatically.

"What happened?" Seth asked, trying to pry

Roxy's fingers off of his arm.

"Something's in there," Roxy said. "Something . . . evil."

"Did you see the monster?" Andy asked, a look of terror in his eyes.

"I caught only a glimpse," Roxy answered, doing her best to look as afraid as Andy. "A darkness. And then I felt icy fingers of terror reach in and grab my heart. I couldn't move. No escape. I couldn't breathe . . ."

Roxy gave an exaggerated cough. Andy looked more scared than ever.

"I told you guys! I told you!" he cried.

Roxy tried not to smile. She knew she had them. She just had to take it one step further. "It had control of my mind," Roxy went on. "I heard its terrible voice, whispering in my head, telling me what it wanted . . ."

"What does it want?" Seth asked, his eyes wide.

Roxy paused. "It wants . . . children," she said in a low and spooky voice.

The boys stared at Roxy for a brief moment, frozen.

Then, at the same moment, they turned and ran back for the field.

Roxy watched them go. A smile crept over her face.

"Suckers," she said.

Brains—and a little overacting—could win out over baseball bats any day!

Chapter Eight:
• • • Secrets • • •

Dinner at the Moody Mansion that night was unusually quiet. Susan was thinking about Jon. Max was thinking about Jill. And Roxy was thinking about Swiftfoot, the shaman, and the girl from the northern lights.

"Does anyone know where the cheese went?" Susan asked, breaking the silence. "I wanted to have it with the cauliflower."

Roxy shrugged. "Beats me," she said casually, knowing she'd fed it to Swiftfoot.

There was more quiet for a while. Susan spoke again.

"So, Jill wasn't here for very long today," she told Max.

"She was just picking up her homework," Max said.

He hadn't meant to let that slip, but Roxy caught it right away. "You did her homework for her?" she asked in disbelief.

Max blushed. "No, no. I . . . just had her book by accident," he lied.

"Good," Roxy said. "Because if you're going to leave me at the altar, I hope it's not for the type of girl who gets you to do her homework for her."

No one spoke again for a while. This time, Max spoke up.

"Where's Jon?" he asked Susan. "Isn't it movie night?"

"Oh, something came up," Susan lied. "He had to cancel."

"What came up?" Roxy asked.

"He didn't really say," Susan said quickly.

That was the last thing any of them said at dinner.

The next morning, Roxy was back at day camp. Ms. Slausen was getting ready to show an educational film.

"In today's documentary, we're going to learn all about photosynthesis," she told the campers. "Remember, no gum or candy in the projection room."

But Roxy had other plans for that day, and they didn't include learning about plants. While the other campers filed into the projection room, she flattened herself against a bookcase.

She was going to make a break for it . . .

While Roxy planned her escape, her mom was planning to make a break of her own. She was leaving Lenny's Coffee Shop, a cup in her hand, when Jon hurried toward her.

"Hey!" he said.

"Oh, hi," Susan replied.

"Listen," Jon began. "I just wanted to know if everything is okay. You seem kind of distant lately."

"Distant? No, not at all," Susan said. But her voice said otherwise.

"Okay, okay," Jon said. "Just checking."

Susan hesitated for a moment. Then she sighed.

"Jon, you're a great guy," she said. "And Roxy just adores you. But . . . you see . . ."

"Wait," Jon said, a little shocked. "Are you dumping me?"

"No!" Susan replied. "No, I just feel things are moving a little too quickly. And I just want to put them on . . . pause for a bit."

"'Pause'?" Jon asked. "Isn't that like 'stop'?"

"Oh, no, not at all," Susan told him. "Stop is stop, and pause is . . . different. I just need some time to think things through. You know?"

"Oh yeah," Jon said, trying to sound like this didn't bother him. "Absolutely. Sure."

Susan looked surprised. "Really?"

"You take as much time as you need," Jon said gently.

Susan smiled, relieved. "Thanks, Jon. I'm so glad you understand," she said. She looked at her watch. "I should get back. I'll see you later."

Jon watched her walk away. Ramma stepped outside.

"I don't think she pressed 'pause,' my friend," he said. "I think she pressed 'eject.'"

· · · ♥ · · ·

Nearby, in town hall, Deputy Sheriff Potts was in Mayor Bloomberg's office.

"I just need to get a couple measurements of the crystal," Potts was saying. "I tell you, when the Serenity Falls Lighthouse is lit up, it's going to be so beautiful."

The mayor worked the dials on the safe. "You know, if it's that beautiful, a speech might get in the way," he said hopefully.

He unlocked the safe. Then he froze.

"Oh no," he said weakly. "It's impossible! I locked it in there myself!"

"What is it?" Potts asked.

Bloomberg staggered back to reveal the inside of the safe.

It was completely empty. The crystal was gone!

"*Noooooooo!*" Potts cried.

Chapter Nine:
• • • The Stolen Crystal • • •

Roxy made a break from the library and headed to the woods. She found Swiftfoot and the shaman at the campsite.

The shaman nodded when he saw Roxy, then continued working on the strange machine. Roxy sat on a fallen log and took some food she had brought with her from her knapsack. As she made sandwiches, she studied the machine.

In the daylight, it looked even more amazing than before. Roxy couldn't even imagine what it was supposed to do. But she knew it had to be something important.

"I still can't believe you built all this," she told the shaman.

The shaman was shifting through a pile of junk. He picked up a piece of glass and tossed it away. Nothing in the pile seemed to satisfy him.

"Running out of time . . ." he muttered.

"Just to make sure we're both on the same page, this is the ceremony about the girl from the northern lights, right?" Roxy asked.

The shaman turned to her, his eyes wide with excitement.

"Yes! Yes! The girl! She has to come!" he cried. "The lights!"

"I knew it!" Roxy said triumphantly.

The shaman turned back to his pile of junk.

"As your apprentice, I should probably know when the ceremony is supposed to begin," Roxy continued.

"She's coming . . . Saturday, nine P.M.," the shaman answered without looking up.

Then he picked up a piece of mirror and held it up, smiling.

"Perfect!" he said.

"Yay!" Roxy cried, clapping her hands. "Uh, what's perfect?"

The shaman walked over to the platform and carefully placed the mirror among the other mirrors there. Then he hurried over to his big cloth sack. He pulled out an object wrapped in an American flag. He gently unraveled the cloth.

Then he held up what was wrapped inside—a large crystal.

Roxy stared, stunned. She had seen that crystal before. It was supposed to be locked up in the mayor's office.

"Where did you get that?" she asked.

"Found it," the shaman answered. "Found it. The house in the ground. Found it."

He carried the crystal over to the platform. Roxy followed him, frowning.

"That's the light thingy for the Serenity Falls Lighthouse," she told him. "I don't think you're supposed to have that. Are you sure you found it?"

"Yes," the shaman insisted. "The house in the ground. Found it."

He carefully placed the crystal on the platform.

"The prismatic nexus," he muttered. "Focal distributor . . ."

Roxy wasn't sure what to think. She looked around the campsite. The American flag caught her eye.

She flashed back to the visit from Deputy Sheriff Potts.

"There were some flags stolen," she whispered. She felt terrible. Was her shaman really a thief? He couldn't be.

She picked up her knapsack. "I'm going to go home now," she said quietly.

The shaman didn't even notice her go.

Roxy hurried as quickly as she could back to the library. She wanted to get there before Sauerkraut Slausen noticed she was gone.

As she approached the sheriff's office, she saw a pickup truck parked outside. Deputy Potts stood in the bed of the truck. He was talking to a small crowd gathered in front of him.

"The Serenity Falls Lighthouse is more than just a symbol of this fine town," he was saying. "And I, for one, am not going to let those thieves shatter the crystal heart of our sesquicentennial."

He pointed to a man in the crowd. "Bob, you and Larry take everything west of Stony Creek. I'll take the East Woods and the Black Marsh. Sam, you—"

Then a bunch of teenagers ran up.

"Wait a second, Deputy! We want in!" one of them called out.

"Oh no," Roxy whispered.

She wasn't sure if the shaman was a thief or not. But she knew in her heart that he was kind. He wouldn't hurt anybody.

But if everyone in town was searching the woods, someone would find him. And the crystal. They would probably put him in jail.

Maybe she should tell the sheriff what she knew. Or maybe she should warn the shaman. Roxy sighed.

For the first time in a long time, Roxy Hunter had no idea what to do next.

Chapter Ten:
· · · Guy Talk · · ·

Max sat in Lenny's Coffee Shop once again, waiting for Jill. He stared at the door, waiting for her to walk in. He could almost picture her smiling at him the way she did . . .

Max took another sip of his milk shake. He looked at his watch. She was late, but that didn't mean anything. She'd probably walk in any minute now . . .

"Hey, Maxie!"

Max smiled as Jill ran in through the door of the coffee shop.

"Did you hear about the lighthouse?" Jill asked.

Max nodded. "Yeah."

"Well, a bunch of us are going to join the search party and try to find the gang of criminals that stole the crystal," Jill said. She had a pleading look on her face. "So . . . oh, I hate asking this . . ."

"You want me to do your homework," Max finished for her, his voice flat.

"Would you? Oh, thanks, Maxie. You're the best!" Jill said.

She blew Max a kiss; then she hurried out the door.

Max sighed. He reached down to the seat beside him and picked up a bunch of flowers.

Max shook his head. He felt really stupid. What was he thinking, anyway? Jill was much older than he was, and really pretty. He tossed the flowers on the table.

Just then Jon walked into the coffee shop. He saw the sad look on Max's face. Then he saw the flowers on the table. He walked over.

"Hey, Max," he said.

"Hey," Max replied glumly.

"Who're the flowers for?" Jon asked.

Max sighed. "Nobody."

Then Jon noticed the French books on the table. He figured out what was going on.

"Mind if I sit down?" he asked.

Max shrugged.

Jon sat. "You know, if you want to talk, I do

have a bit of experience with relationships—not all of it good," he said.

Max looked at Jon. "She took my heart," he said sadly. "But all she gave me was her homework."

Jon nodded. "Well, these things are complex," he said. "For example, let me tell you what happened to Susan and me . . ."

Before he could stop himself, Jon poured out his heart to Max. Max listened patiently. He was relieved he wasn't the one who had to talk.

"And then she tells me I bought the wrong confetti!" Jon was ranting. "Tell me, Max, is there a right kind of confetti? And this whole 'pause' thing—what the heck is 'pause'? I haven't been rushing things. I've been taking it slow. If I go any slower, I'll start collecting dust! I mean, I don't know what to do!"

"Whoa! Slow down," Max said, chuckling. He thought for a moment and then continued. "Maybe that's the problem."

"What?" Jon asked.

"Taking it too slow. Last winter, I taught Roxy how to skate," Max began. "She fell down and hurt herself and swore she would never skate again. And you know how stubborn she can be."

Jon nodded. "Oh, yeah."

"Well, I could have stood there for hours telling her how much fun skating was, but instead, I picked her up and just started skating with her," Max continued. "By the end of the day, I couldn't get her off the ice."

"You're losing me, buddy," Jon said.

"Susan has good reason to be afraid of getting hurt," Max reminded him. "She lost her husband."

Jon finally understood. "So, instead of talking about it, I should show her that skating is fun."

Max nodded. He was glad Jon was too distracted by his own problems to talk about Max's anymore!

"Boy, I'm glad we had this chat!" Jon said with a sigh of relief.

. . . ♥ . . .

While Jon and Max talked, Roxy snuck back into the library. She didn't want Ms. Slausen to see her just yet. She still had thinking to do.

Roxy crawled under Mr. Tibers's desk. The librarian found her a few minutes later. He bent down to look at her.

"Ms. Hunter, I won't venture to ask what

you're doing down there, but are you aware that Ms. Slausen has been looking for you?" Mr. Tibers asked.

"I needed a time-out from the cut-and-paste academy," Roxy told him. "I've got a lot on my mind."

Mr. Tibers gave a knowing nod. He crouched down next to her. "Is it regarding your mother and Jon?" he asked.

"No," Roxy replied. "What about them?"

"Oh, nothing," Mr. Tibers said quickly. "Nothing at all. What is it then?"

Roxy sighed. "Did you ever find yourself in a situation where you didn't know if you had to do the wrong thing for the right reason, or the right thing for the wrong reason? Because either way, it's going to have reepercushions."

"Ms. Hunter, you're being a little obtuse," the librarian said.

"Of course I'm obtusing," Roxy said, exasperated. "I can't tell you what it is."

The librarian thought for a moment. "Well, sometimes, regardless of how you feel, you have to do what you know is right," he said. "Despite the *repercussions*."

"Yeah, I was afraid you'd say that," Roxy

said. She crawled out from under the desk.

"Mr. Tibers, I've got to go do something," she announced. "Could you keep Sauerkraut off my back?"

The librarian smiled. "With pleasure!" he said.

Chapter Eleven:
• • • Captured • • •

Roxy knew exactly where to find her mom. The sesquicentennial celebration was keeping her busy. Susan was in the town park, decorating the gazebo with red, white, and blue streamers.

"Hey, hon," Susan said when she saw her daughter. "Why aren't you at day camp?"

"I've got to talk to you about something, Mom," Roxy said.

Susan heard the sadness in Roxy's voice. "Oh, honey. Did someone tell you? Seems like everybody knows," she said.

"They do?" Roxy asked, puzzled.

"It's these small towns—so gossipy," Susan said. She knelt down and looked into Roxy's eyes. "I know you really like him. And I do, too. Besides, it's not a breakup. We're just taking some time."

Suddenly Roxy knew what her mom was talking about. "You dumped Jon?" she asked.

"No, no," Susan protested. "We're just on pause."

"Pause?" Roxy asked. "What the heck is 'pause'?"

"Well, it's kind of hard to explain," Susan said.

Roxy's mind was reeling. She wanted to know more, but she had to do what she had come to do.

"This isn't about you and Jon," she said. "I have something I have to tell you."

A look of worry crossed Susan's face. "What?" she asked.

"Well . . ." Roxy began, but she was interrupted by Mayor Bloomberg. He came running toward the gazebo.

"Wonderful news, Susan!" he cried. "They found the crystal!"

"What!" Roxy cried. It was exactly as she had feared. "Where?"

"In the woods," the mayor answered. "Some vagrant type had stolen it. How he got into that safe will have me forever flummoxed."

"Vagrant type?" Roxy felt awful. They must be talking about the shaman.

"They're just bringing him in to the sheriff's station," Mayor Bloomberg said.

"Oh no!" Roxy cried. She jumped off the gazebo and ran toward the sheriff's.

"Roxy! Where are you going?" Susan called after her.

Roxy didn't answer. Susan dropped the crepe paper and followed.

• • • ♥ • • •

As Roxy reached the sheriff's station, she saw a crowd of people gathered outside. Sheriff Tom stood on top of the front steps. Beside him, in handcuffs, was the shaman.

"Put him in jail! He's a thief!" one of the men in the crowd cried out.

"Gotta go," the shaman mumbled. "Not much time." He started to walk down the steps, but the sheriff grabbed his arms.

"Just wait right there, sir. You're not going anywhere," he said. Then he turned to the townspeople. "People! People! Simmer down! We are going to resolve this in an orderly fashion. But I want everyone to calm down first."

The angry crowd quieted.

"Thank you," the sheriff said.

Then Roxy burst onto the scene. "He's innocent!" she yelled.

Everyone looked at her.

"He didn't do it!" Roxy said passionately. "He's a shaman. A native mystic. And he's performing a sacred ceremony."

Susan arrived, and Roxy turned to her mother.

"Mom, he's innocent," Roxy said. "He told me he found the crystal in the ground. And I believe him."

Susan looked shocked.

"Roxy, you know this man?" she asked.

"Yes, I'm his apprentice," Roxy said.

Susan went pale. "What?"

"He's teaching me the ceremony of the northern lights," Roxy said.

Her mother looked worried and angry at the same time.

"Roxy, we're going home," she said softly but firmly.

"But, Ma—" Roxy pleaded.

"Now!" Susan yelled. She cast a pleading look at the sheriff. Tears formed in her eyes.

"Don't worry, Susan," he said. "I'll get to the bottom of this."

Roxy looked down at her sneakers. She had tried to do the right thing. But she was too late. Now *everything* had gone wrong. There was nothing more she could do.

The shaman was captured. The ceremony of the northern lights would never happen. The girl from the stars—or New Jersey—would never appear.

And she was in big, big trouble.

Roxy tries to strike up a partnership with her favorite author, Lorne Red Deer

Roxy meets Swiftfoot, her new sidekick

Sheriff Potts visits the Hunters to let them know about a string of thefts

Roxy comes face-to-face with the Marsh Monster

Roxy is amazed by the Shaman's creation

Roxy protects Swiftfoot and the Shaman from the local bullies with her wild imagination

Roxy defends the Shaman

Max and Swiftfoot hunt for clues in the Black Marsh

Roxy bakes a cake (with a file inside!) to help the Shaman escape from jail

Some people will do anything to look young!

Roxy arrives at the jail, only to find that the Shaman has already escaped!

The whole town searches the forest for the Shaman and Roxy

It's almost time!

The Shaman's invention worked!

Roxy stands in the light, but the Shaman sees his daughter, Sarah, and finally has the chance to say good-bye

The Serenity Falls Sesquicentennial Celebration

Another case closed by Roxy Hunter!

Chapter Twelve:
· · · Grounded for Life · · ·

That night, Roxy lay on her bed, staring at the ceiling.

"Princess Roxahana lies on her bed, awaiting the executioner's call," she moaned dramatically. Her mom hadn't told her exactly how much trouble she was in yet, and the waiting was terrible. In fact, her mom had barely spoken to her at all, and that was even worse.

She heard a gentle knock on the door.

"Here we go," she said under her breath. Then she raised her voice. "Come in."

The door opened, and Max entered.

"What's the sentence?" Roxy asked him.

"Grounded for life. No chance of parole," Max said only half jokingly.

"I don't see what the big deal is," Roxy protested.

"Being out in the woods at night was strike number one," Max told her. "Let alone with a stranger. Do you know how bad that is?"

"How bad?" Roxy asked.

"Bad," Max replied.

"Scale of one to ten?" Roxy tried.

"Fifteen," Max said.

Roxy sighed. "Is she still angry?"

"Well, I think she's more disappointed than angry," Max said carefully.

Roxy flopped back down on her bed. "Oh. Disappointed. That's worse."

"Roxy, think about it," Max said. "What if something had happened to you?"

"Yeah, I guess," Roxy said quietly.

"Good night," Max said. He left the room, closing the door behind him.

Roxy felt tears well up in her eyes. She hadn't even thought how worried her mom might be.

· · · ♥ · · ·

Over at the sheriff's station, Sheriff Tom and Deputy Potts went through a bag of the shaman's belongings. They found some strange things, like photo lenses and mirrors. And they found some personal things, too, like a beat-up wedding ring and an old photo of a little girl. The photo was tattered around the edges, but the little girl still smiled brightly—she looked just like the shaman.

"This doesn't look like any thief to me," Sheriff Tom said. "How did he manage to get into that safe? No lock picks, no skeleton keys, nothing."

"He swallowed them!" Potts suggested.

"What?" Sheriff Tom asked.

"Like Harry Houdini," Potts explained. "He used to swallow his lock pick and barf it up when he needed it. Maybe our guy is an escape artist."

The sheriff sighed patiently. His deputy wasn't exactly the smartest guy in town, but now he just sounded silly.

"Well, we're not going to get an ID on his prints until morning," Sheriff Tom said. "Maybe you'd like to escape for the night, Bull."

"Gotcha, boss," Potts said.

The sheriff watched Potts leave. He picked up the tattered photo, curious.

Down the hall, in the holding cell, the shaman

paced back and forth like a caged animal. He stopped and gripped the bars.

"Not much time," he muttered. "Not much time."

· · · ♥ · · ·

The next morning dawned, and Serenity Falls turned 150 years old. When Jon walked into Lenny's Coffee Shop, he found Ramma wearing giant red, white, and blue glasses. A foam Statue of Liberty crown sat on top of his brown hair.

"Happy Sesquicentennial!" Ramma cried. He held up his arm, pretending to hold the Statue of Liberty's torch. "Guess who I am?"

"Elton John hailing a cab?" Jon guessed.

Ramma lowered his arm, frowning. "That is the third time I have heard that."

Jon walked over to the counter. Sheriff Tom sat there, sipping a cup of coffee.

"Hey there, Jon," the sheriff said. "Listen, I heard about you and Susan. Real shame. I was rootin' for you two."

"Yeah, well, it ain't over till it's over," Jon replied with determination. "Did you get an ID on our thief?"

The sheriff nodded. "Came in this morning,"

he said. "Gerard Rossi. Couple arrests for vagrancy but nothing else. Seems harmless enough. Left a message with a relative over in Mansfield. He's gonna come by tonight."

Sheriff Tom paused. "I'll be honest with you. This whole mess doesn't sit right with me."

. . . ♥ . . .

By afternoon, Susan and Roxy were speaking again—mostly about how punished Roxy was. For starters, she wasn't even allowed to go to the sesquicentennial celebration.

Roxy sat at the kitchen table, eating a peanut-butter sandwich. She watched Susan and Max rush around the kitchen, getting ready to go.

"All right, I still have a million things to do," Susan said. "I have to go arrange the deejay booth, then pick up the punch . . ."

"I can pick up the punch," Max offered.

Susan flashed Max a grateful smile. "You're a savior. Thanks."

"You know, Mom, it seems kind of sad that I won't be able to appreciate all the hard work you've put into this dance," Roxy said casually.

"Nice try," her mom replied.

Just then, the doorbell rang.

"That's the babysitter," Susan said. She ran off to get the door.

Roxy looked at Max. "You know, I may have done something wrong, but the shaman didn't. He said he found that dumb thing in a house in the ground, and I believe him."

"So do I," Max said.

Roxy was startled. "You do?"

"Logically, it doesn't add up," Max reasoned. "How would he have been able to break into the mayor's office, unlock the safe, and steal the crystal? Furthermore, how would he have even known it was there?"

Max paused. There was something more that had to be said. "Besides, something else points to his innocence. You may do some dumb things, Roxy, but you do judge character well."

"I do?" Roxy said.

"Yeah," Max replied sadly. "You were right about Jill."

Roxy got up from her seat and hugged Max.

"Oh, Max, you believe me! I never gave up hope on us," she said. Then she looked at Max quizzically. "So, who did steal it?"

"I have no idea," Max said. Then he looked over Roxy's shoulder. "Your babysitter's here."

Roxy didn't like the look on Max's face. She turned around.

Standing in the kitchen doorway was Sauerkraut Slausen!

Chapter Thirteen:
• • • Roxy's Plan • • •

Max arrived at the town gazebo later that afternoon. He carried a cardboard box in his arms and dangled a big garbage bag from one hand.

"Here's the punch mix," he told Susan. He plunked down his packages.

"Thanks, Max," Susan said. She nodded toward the bag. "What's this?"

"It's from Jon," Max replied. "He told me to give it to you."

Curious, Susan opened the bag. It was filled with red, white, and blue confetti. She smiled.

"If you don't need me for anything else, I have some things to do," Max said.

"What?" Susan said, lost in thought. "Oh yeah. Sure. Thanks."

Back at the Moody Mansion, Roxy was working on a plan.

She didn't want to get into any more trouble. But she had to help the shaman. He didn't deserve to be in jail.

Roxy had asked Ms. Slausen if she could bake a cake. That was fine with the babysitter. She sat at the dining room table, reading a magazine, while Roxy worked.

It didn't take long for Roxy to turn the kitchen into a disaster area. Flour powdered the walls. Eggshells littered the table. Butter stained the counters. The result of the mess was a big, round cake that Roxy pulled out of the oven. She dumped it out of the pan, onto the table.

Then Roxy picked up a big carpenter's file she had found in the basement. She carefully slid the file into the cake.

"Perfect," Roxy muttered. In old movies, the file-in-a-cake trick worked every time. She just had to deliver the cake to the shaman. Then he'd find the file and use it to cut the bars of his jail cell. She'd be home before anyone knew she was gone.

Now she just had to cover the evidence. She reached for a big bowl of frosting. She stuck her hand in and lifted up a big blob. Then she started smearing it on the cake.

"Oh, please, like I believe that!" Ms. Slausen's voice carried into the kitchen from the other room.

Roxy walked to the dining room door. "Whatever is troubling you, Ms. Slausen?" she asked in her sweetest voice.

"What a bunch of horse hooey," Ms. Slausen said, nodding at her magazine. "They take a picture of some eighteen-year-old and tell us we'll look like that if we shell out fifty dollars. Well, I did, and all I got was a bottle of useless goop."

Roxy looked at her icing-covered hand. An idea formed in her mind.

"You're right, that's criminal," Roxy agreed. "I mean, I know for a fact that the only thing that truly works is my mother's secret Chinese botanical ointment."

Ms. Slausen raised an eyebrow, curious. "What?"

"Oops!" Roxy said. "I'm not supposed to mention it. Forget I said anything."

"No, no, you can tell me, dear," Ms. Slausen said eagerly.

"Are you sure?" Roxy asked.

"Of course," the babysitter replied. "I can keep a secret."

"Cross your heart?" Roxy asked.

Ms. Slausen drew an *X* over her heart with her finger. "Absolutely," she promised.

Roxy tried to keep from smiling. Her plan was working even better than she'd hoped. Her brain quickly spun a tale.

"Well, my great-great-grandfather, the famed explorer Horatio Hunter III, brought the secret recipe back from the So Yung Province of China," Roxy said. "He got it from a medicine woman who claimed to be one hundred and twenty. He said she didn't look a day over fifty."

Ms. Slausen looked skeptical. "Oh, I don't believe that," she said.

Roxy shrugged. "How old do you think my mom is?"

"Early thirties," Ms. Slausen answered.

Roxy leaned in toward Ms. Slausen. "She's forty-seven."

"No!" Ms. Slausen exclaimed.

"Would I lie?" Roxy asked.

The babysitter was hooked now. "Does she have any?"

"Why? Do you want to try it?" asked Roxy.

"Yes!" Ms. Slausen cried. Then she realized she might seem too eager. "I mean, I'd be curious."

Roxy paused for dramatic effect. "Well . . . maybe this one time."

Minutes later, Roxy had Ms. Slausen stretched out on the couch, surrounded by pillows and blankets. She put some soothing music on the CD player. The babysitter closed her eyes, and Roxy gently smeared cake icing all over her face.

"It tastes sweet," Ms. Slausen said, sticking out her tongue a little.

"Just think how sweet your skin will be," Roxy promised. She used up the last bit of icing. "Now, the secret is, you mustn't move, otherwise the nutriments won't be absorbed. Just relax and concentrate on your breathing."

"You mean *nutrients*, dear," Ms. Slausen corrected her.

Roxy placed two cucumber slices over Ms. Slausen's eyes.

"Yes, ma'am. Now think beautiful thoughts," Roxy added.

Ms. Slausen squirmed a little. "Well, this is—"

"No, no!" Roxy cut her off. "You mustn't talk. Or move. Just lie there and relax. Relaaaaaax . . ."

The babysitter took a deep breath. Roxy smiled.

Then she tiptoed out of the room.

She had a jailbreak to plan.

· · · ♥ · · ·

Meanwhile, Max was working on a plan of his own. He walked to the shaman's old campsite and stared at the strange machine.

A stationary bike made up part of the machine. Max stepped on one of the pedals. As it turned, a spark shot out from one of the car batteries attached to the contraption.

"Hmmmm," Max said. He looked up at the trees, in the direction the machine was pointing. Afternoon sunlight lit up all the mirrors and glass pieces dangling from the branches.

"Impressive," Max said, nodding.

Just then, Swiftfoot came into the campsite. He stopped, cautious.

"Hello, dog," Max said. He held out his hand. Swiftfoot slowly approached. He sniffed Max's hand. Then his tail began to wag. He sat down and offered his paw to Max. Max laughed and shook it.

"Nice to meet you," Max said.

Max took his hand away. It was covered in

mud. Curious, he looked down at the ground. It was dry.

Then Max sniffed the mud. It smelled strong.

A clue, Max thought. An idea was beginning to percolate in his brain. He walked around the campsite. He stopped by the shaman's junk sack.

The sack was streaked with mud. Max sniffed it, and it had the same strong smell.

Max nodded. He looked around some more and saw a trail heading into the woods. He turned to Swiftfoot.

"Come on, boy," Max said.

Then Max and the dog headed down the trail.

Chapter Fourteen:
• • • The Truth Uncovered • • •

Roxy entered the sheriff's office, carrying her cake. She had expected to have to charm the sheriff or his deputy, but neither man was there.

"Hello?" Roxy called.

There was no reply. Roxy tried again.

"Anybody here?"

Roxy breathed a sigh of relief. This was going to be easier than she had thought. She ran down the hallway toward the holding cell.

The hall and the cell were both dark. Roxy peered through the metal bars.

But the cell was empty.

Roxy gasped. Had they taken the shaman somewhere? But then she noticed that the cell door was open slightly. She took a step back . . . right into the shaman!

"*Aaaaaaaah!*" Roxy screamed.

"*Aaaaaaaah!*" screamed the shaman.

Roxy dropped the cake, and it fell to the floor.

"How did you get out?" she asked. Then it dawned on her. "You *are* magic!"

"No time!" the shaman said hurriedly. He pushed past Roxy, heading down the hallway.

Roxy followed him to the sheriff's office. The shaman began searching through the papers on the sheriff's desk. Then he started opening drawers.

"No time. No time," he said.

"Come on, we have to make a break for it!" Roxy said, panicked.

But the shaman kept searching. Roxy had no idea what he was doing. He could be free—free! But not if he stayed here.

"They could be back any second!" Roxy warned. "We have to go!"

Finally the shaman pulled a plastic bag out of one of the drawers. It had his things in it. He took out a photograph and held it up—it was the photo of a little girl.

"What is that?" Roxy asked.

The shaman hesitated. Then he handed the photo to Roxy.

96

"Sarah," he said.

Roxy took it. The girl in the photo was about her age, with long hair. But the photo looked old and tattered.

"Sarah?" Roxy asked.

"Sarah," the shaman said. "She's the light. Gone."

"Is Sarah your daughter?" Roxy asked.

The shaman nodded. The truth slowly dawned on Roxy.

"And you . . . you lost her?" Roxy asked, her voice soft.

The shaman looked down sadly.

"And the lights," Roxy said. "You think she'll come if she sees them."

The shaman nodded. "The lights. She'll come to the lights."

Roxy understood. The shaman wasn't magic. He was just a man, a sad man who had lost his young daughter. And he wanted to bring her back.

Roxy knew how he felt.

"Yeah, I know what you mean," she said. "After my dad died, I used to write him little notes and attach them to balloons. I'd let them go up into the sky so he could read them. It helped a lot."

Roxy looked at the shaman's sad face. Now she wanted to help him more than ever.

"You need that crystal," Roxy said.

"The prismatic nexus," the shaman explained.

Roxy took a deep breath. Sometimes you have to do the right thing for the wrong reasons. And sometimes you have to do the wrong thing for the right reasons.

In her heart, Roxy knew this was the right thing to do.

"Meet me at the campsite," she said.

The shaman looked unsure.

Roxy looked into his dark eyes. "Trust me."

· · · ♥ · · ·

Max followed the trail away from the campsite and into the marsh. The ground below his feet was damp and muddy. He leaned down and picked up some of the mud. It smelled just like the mud on the shaman's bag.

He was in the right place.

Swiftfoot had wandered away from his side. Max watched the dog ramble along the trees bordering the marsh. Max followed the dog.

"It's around here, isn't it?" Max asked.

Swiftfoot trotted over to a mound of earth

behind a fallen tree. Max walked over. He cleared away a bunch of branches.

Underneath was a latch. Max pulled on it, and a door in the ground creaked open.

Max took a flashlight out of his jacket. He shone it into the dark opening.

"A house in the ground," he whispered, echoing Roxy's words.

Max bravely stepped into the underground chamber.

In his bones, he knew that's where the truth would be found.

Chapter Fifteen:
· · · A Race Against Time · · ·

The sun set over Serenity Falls. People gathered around the gazebo in the center of town. The red, white, and blue streamers were all hung, and the lighthouse sat behind a curtain on the gazebo, waiting to be unveiled at the official ceremony. The large crystal sat on top of the lighthouse.

Acting Mayor Saul Bloomberg paced nervously behind the curtain. He was practicing his speech.

"Good evening, ladies and gentlemen," he said in an unsure voice. "I was told to open with a joke . . ."

Just then, Roxy stepped behind the curtain.

"Hello, Mayor Bloomberg," she said. "You don't look so good."

"I feel terrible," the mayor moaned. "What's my joke? I can't remember my joke. My brain's gone numb!"

Roxy thought quickly. She had to get her hands on that crystal. But she couldn't do anything with the mayor there.

Then she had an idea.

"Don't worry," she told him. "It's just the local news."

"Local news?" Bloomberg sounded panicked. "What do you mean?"

"The television crew that just pulled up," Roxy said innocently.

Bloomberg began to sweat. "Television crew?"

"No one really watches it," Roxy said. "Unless it gets picked up nationally. You know how those big networks love stories from small-town America."

The mayor's face practically turned green. "I don't feel so good," he said.

Then he ran off.

Roxy looked around. The coast was clear. It was just her and the crystal.

If she was going to act, it had to be now.

Back in the marsh, Max bravely made his way into the hole in the ground. It appeared to be some kind of old bomb shelter, he reasoned. He shone his flashlight around. There was nothing really scary about it, just some cobwebs, dusty boxes, and a rotting couch.

Max slowly circled the shelter, shining his light in every corner. If his hunch was right, there should be more here than just cobwebs.

Then he saw what he was looking for. A pile of American flags, surrounding a stone eagle.

"From the library," Max said.

Then the flashlight lit up something on the ground. Something small and yellow.

Something clicked in Max's brain. It was like the pieces of a puzzle were coming together.

He knew who the real thief was!

Back at the gazebo, Sheriff Tom stood in front of the curtain. The townspeople gathered in front of him, waiting for the unveiling of the lighthouse.

"Again, I'd like to wish Acting Mayor Bloomberg a speedy recovery," the sheriff was saying. "And now, without further ado, ladies and gents, I give you the Serenity Falls Lighthouse!"

He pulled open the curtain. The lighthouse stood there—but the crystal was gone! A gasp of shock ran through the crowd.

Just then Deputy Potts ran up. He clutched his head as though he were hurt.

"He escaped!" the deputy cried. "The crystal thief escaped!"

Sheriff Tom looked at the empty space above the lighthouse. "Looks like he's struck again."

The sheriff took Deputy Potts back to the station and got an ice pack for his head. He tried to get the story of what had happened from his deputy.

"So, he cracked you with your own nightstick?" the sheriff asked. He didn't sound convinced. "What is he, a ninja?"

"He's fast, boss," Potts said.

Jon walked into the office.

"Hey, Tom, there's a crowd forming out there," he said. "They're going out to the woods to look for the guy."

"Yeah, I was afraid of that," the sheriff replied. "Bull and I will go along and keep an eye on them."

Then Susan ran in, panicked.

"Sheriff! I just heard from Mayor Bloomberg that Roxy was the last person he saw near the lighthouse!" she cried.

Sheriff Tom rubbed his temples. "Oh, boy," he said. "Let's go, Bull."

"I'm going with you," Susan said firmly.

"Me too," Jon added.

. . . ♥ . . .

Roxy ran through the woods, cradling the crystal in her arms. She leaped over fallen branches. She pushed through the underbrush.

She had to get there fast. Before it was too late.

When she arrived at the campsite, the shaman was tinkering with his machine. Roxy ran up to him and handed him the crystal.

"I got it!" she cried.

He took it from her without a word, then carried it to the platform. He carefully set it in place.

"We'd better hurry," Roxy urged. "This is the first place they'll come looking for us."

She looked at her watch. It was almost nine o'clock.

"We're running out of time!" Roxy cried.

Chapter Sixteen:
• • • The Shaman's Lights • • •

A crowd of townspeople crashed through
the woods. Sheriff Tom and Deputy Potts led the
way. Their flashlights shone through the trees,
illuminating the trail ahead.

Susan and Jon walked side by side.

"Don't worry," Jon said. "She'll be okay."

Susan looked at him, grateful for the
support.

She just hoped Jon was right.

Then a voice called out from the crowd.

"It's over here! I see it!"

The people in the crowd began to talk
excitedly.

"Everybody calm down!" Sheriff Tom called
out. "I don't want anyone to get hurt!"

But most of the people ignored him. They

surged ahead, running toward the camp.

Sheriff Tom shook his head. "This is gonna get ugly," he sighed. He broke into a run.

Susan panicked.

"Oh no! Roxy!" she cried.

She and Jon charged ahead.

Back at the campsite, the shaman sat on the stationary bike. Roxy watched as he pedaled furiously.

"Nothing's happening," Roxy said, worried.

Then she heard voices in the distance. It sounded like a crowd of people were coming toward them. She looked into the trees and saw flashlight beams moving back and forth.

"They're going to be here any second!" she cried.

The shaman pedaled faster and faster. Soon he was drenched in sweat. A crackle of electricity danced along the coils of the machine, snapping across the batteries.

Roxy saw the mob break through the tree line.

"They're here!" she yelled. "It's too late! It's nine o'clock!"

The mob ran at them. The shaman jumped off the bike, then dived to a connecting lever. He pulled the switch.

Boom!

A loud noise echoed through the woods. An intense beam of light shot from the machine. It hit the crystal directly.

The crystal split the light into countless rays. They shot into the trees, reflecting off the dangling mirrors and glass. The light danced in the branches. It looked like the shaman had brought the heavens down into the woods.

The angry mob stopped and stared, mouths agape. They looked in stunned silence at the beautiful light show. Susan gasped and grabbed Jon's hand, squeezing it tightly.

Then the light did an amazing thing. All of the beams bounced off the reflectors and merged into a single beam of light. The light shot straight down into the ground.

Roxy stared at the beam, transfixed. She had never seen anything so beautiful before. Slowly she walked toward the beam. Then she stopped in the middle of it, closing her eyes. She let the soft pink light bathe her body.

The shaman looked up. He saw a little girl standing inside the light. But to him, she wasn't Roxy. It was the little girl he had lost years ago, Sarah—his daughter.

He walked toward the light in a daze. Then he fell to his knees.

"You came back," he said, choking down a sob. He reached out and gently touched her face. "I've missed you so much."

Tears streamed down his face. "I just wanted to say . . . good-bye, Sarah."

Roxy looked down at the shaman, her heart breaking as he put his head in his hands and sobbed.

Then sparks flew from the rack of batteries.

The lights dimmed, then went dark. Roxy put a hand on the shaman's shoulder.

"Are you going to be okay now?" she asked.

He looked up, a sad smile on his face.

"Yes," he said. "Thank you."

Chapter Seventeen:
• • • The Real Thief • • •

The light show had been spectacular. But the shaman was still in trouble—and so was Roxy. Sheriff Tom brought them all back to his station. He handcuffed the shaman to a chair. The crowd of townspeople milled around the lobby, waiting to see what would happen.

Susan and Jon stood by Roxy as she tried to explain things to the sheriff. "But you have to let him go! He just wanted to say good-bye to his daughter. I'm the one who stole the crystal. I should be the one in trouble, not the shaman!"

Sheriff Tom picked up the file from the cake that Roxy had tried to give to the shaman. It still had frosting on it. "We're getting to that," he said, giving her a stern look. "But the fact remains, he assaulted an officer of the law. And he's our prime suspect in the first theft."

"He's innocent!" Roxy insisted. "He said he found it in the ground!"

"That's not possible," Deputy Potts said.

"Yes it is."

They all looked up to see Max standing in the doorway.

"Roxy's right," he said. "This man is innocent."

"How do you know that?" Jon asked.

"I went to the campsite," Max explained. "I found traces of mud there, high in phosphates and nitrates. The only place around here with that kind of mud is found in the Black Marsh. I went there and found an old bomb shelter. The stone eagle from the library and some of the stolen flags were in it."

"He could have been using that as a hiding place," Sheriff Tom said.

"A possibility," Max agreed. "Until I found . . . this."

He held up the clue he had found in the shelter.

A Lemon Boofoo candy wrapper.

"Ramma's the thief?" Roxy asked, puzzled.

"No," Max said. "I remember Ramma telling

112

me that the only person who ate these was Deputy Potts."

Max looked right at the deputy. The crowd gasped.

"Are you saying I did it?" Potts said. "That's ridiculous!"

"No, it's not," Max said firmly. "You had access to the mayor's office, and you knew the combination to the safe. I did a Web search and found that the Black Marsh has been in the Potts family for over a hundred years. My guess is that your grandfather built that bomb shelter during the Cold War and kept it a family secret. You were the only one who knew it was there."

Roxy remembered something, too. "And when I came into the station to rescue the shaman, Deputy Potts wasn't here. He couldn't have been knocked out."

Now all eyes in the room were on Potts. There was a look of fear on his face.

"Do you have anything to say about this, Bull?" Sheriff Tom asked gently.

"I . . . I . . ." Potts began. Then he broke down, blubbering. "I'm sorry. He didn't steal the crystal. I did."

The crowd gasped again.

"I couldn't let an innocent man take the fall for something I did," Potts said, looking down at his shoes. "So I unlocked the cell and left the station. I figured he'd run away. I didn't think he'd go back to the campsite."

"Then how did you get that bump on your head?" Jon asked.

"I hit myself," Potts answered sheepishly.

Sheriff Tom shook his head. "Why in the name of Great-aunt Petunia did you do all this?"

Deputy Potts continued sniffling. "Because I wanted a little respect," he said miserably. "I got so tired of people teasing me and calling me 'Bull.' It was one stupid dance, twenty years ago! I figured if I recovered the stolen crystal, people would think I was a hero. Instead of being a loser named Bull."

Roxy was kind of impressed. "You stole it and hid it so you could be the one to find it? Not bad."

Potts turned to the shaman. "I'm sorry, Mr. Rossi. I didn't mean to put you through this."

The shaman reached out to Potts. He took the deputy's hand.

"It's okay," he said.

Then Potts really broke down. He hugged the

shaman, sobbing again. Jon walked up to them.

"Gee, Martin, we didn't know that name bothered you so much," he said. "Sorry about that."

Potts looked up, his face streaked with tears. "Thanks," he said. He squeezed Jon in a bear hug.

Sheriff Tom looked like he couldn't wait for the night to be over. He turned to the crowd.

"All right, folks. Let's clear out," he announced. "There's an unveiling to get to. I'll sort this out."

As the mob cleared, a man entered the station. Roxy didn't recognize him.

"May I help you, sir?" the sheriff asked him.

"I got a phone call about Gerry Rossi," he said. "I'm his cousin, Bill."

The shaman looked up. Recognition flickered faintly in his eyes.

"Bill?" he asked.

• • • ♥ • • •

Since the shaman was innocent, Sheriff Tom agreed that he could leave with his cousin. After filling Bill in on what happened, the men left the office, followed by Roxy and Susan.

"So, I guess he's not a shaman after all?" Roxy asked Bill.

"Gerry? Not that I know of," Bill answered.

"Then how did he do that magic with the lights?" Roxy asked.

Bill stopped. "You ever see Laser Floyd?"

Roxy's mom nodded. "Of course," Susan said.

"That was Gerry's," Bill explained. "He was a top optical engineer. He used to travel the country designing and building laser light shows."

They arrived at Bill's car. He opened the door for the shaman.

"It's going to be okay, Gerry," he told his cousin. "I'm going to take you home. I'll just be a second."

The shaman got into the car. Bill closed the door. He turned to Susan and Roxy.

"Ten years ago, he was designing a laser show out in Seattle," he said. "He flew his daughter, Sarah, out for it. She was a beautiful little girl."

"The light of his life," Roxy said.

Bill nodded. "Yeah. That's what he used to call her. Anyway, her plane didn't make it. It completely destroyed him. Something in him just snapped. He's been wandering since then. He keeps trying to build these devices, but either the townspeople run him off or he gets arrested for vagrancy."

Bill looked thoughtful. "I guess he just wanted to say good-bye," he said. He looked at Roxy. "And you let him. Thanks so much."

Bill climbed into his car. The shaman—Gerry—rolled down his window. Roxy walked over to him.

"Good-bye, Mr. Rossi," she said.

He reached out of the window and took her hand. "When something comes from the heart, it is magic," he said. "Thank you, Roxy."

Bill drove off, leaving Roxy alone with her mom. Roxy sighed.

"Time to pay the piper," Roxy said softly. She turned to her mom. "Listen, I know I did a bad thing. Okay . . . a lot of bad things. But I want you to know I did them for the right reasons, and . . ."

Roxy stopped. She realized her mom was crying.

"You okay?" she asked.

Susan pulled Roxy close to her. "I love you so much, sweetheart."

"I love you, too, Mom," Roxy said, hugging her mom tightly. She was glad things were back to normal—well, almost normal. Roxy pulled back a little. "Am I still grounded?"

Chapter Eighteen:
• • • Another Case Closed • • •

Stars twinkled in the night sky as the people of Serenity Falls gathered in front of the gazebo once again. Mayor Bloomberg had found some courage and was able to give his speech without sweating too much.

"It is my great honor to present to you, the people of this great community, the Serenity Falls Lighthouse!" he announced. He seemed to surprise himself. "I did it! I made a speech!"

The curtain behind him parted to reveal the lighthouse. This time, the crystal sat on top, shining brightly. It was nice but nothing compared to the light show in the woods.

Roxy and Max watched from the crowd.

"A little anticlimactic," Roxy remarked.

"I'll say," Max agreed.

The unveiling ended with a smattering of fireworks that lit up the sky. They sizzled briefly, then faded. Everyone applauded.

The deejay began to spin some tunes, starting with a mellow dance show. Roxy drifted away from the festivities. She sat on a park bench and stared at the sky.

The shaman had finally said good-bye to his daughter. But a sadness still hung over Roxy. One she couldn't explain.

Susan walked up and sat next to her.

"Hey, pumpkin," she said. "You okay?"

"Yeah, I just . . . I still feel a little achy in my heart. Sometimes I really miss Dad," she said. "But I'm okay."

"I know, honey." Susan brushed a strand of hair from Roxy's face. "Well, would a dance cheer you up?" she asked.

"No thanks, Mom," Roxy said. "Besides, I'm not the one you should be dancing with."

Over by the dancers, Jon, Sheriff Tom, and Max stood on the sidelines.

"I tell you, Jon, you're going to love the single life," the sheriff was saying. "We have bachelor bowling league, fishing, Wednesday-night poker . . ."

Then Susan walked up. She looked at Jon a little shyly.

"Hey, Jon," she said.

"Hey," he said.

"I was wondering if . . . would you like to dance?" she asked.

Jon smiled. "Sure."

She took his hand, and they headed toward the dancers.

Sheriff Tom turned to Max.

"That was some grade-A detecting you did there, Max," he said. "I could use a guy like you on the force."

"Why? You're not firing Deputy Potts, are you?" Max asked.

The sheriff smiled. He looked over at the punch table, where Deputy Potts was hugging Mayor Bloomberg. He hadn't stopped hugging people since his confession.

"Nah. He wasn't trying to hurt anybody," Sheriff Tom said. "Besides, we all have to take some responsibility for calling him 'Bull' all those years. Don't get me wrong. He's going into counseling, and he's gonna do a heck of a lot of community service, but he's a decent fellow at heart."

Then Jill walked up to Max.

"Wanna dance?" she asked him.

"Sure," Max said, shrugging.

Jill led Max to the dance floor. Sheriff Tom looked after them, wistfully.

"Yep," he said. "Bowling and fishing . . ."

On the dance floor, Jon and Susan moved to the music. Susan looked into Jon's eyes.

"Listen, Jon, I owe you an apology," Susan began. "You've been so wonderful. And really, any problems we've had are my fault. Seeing that poor man made me realize that maybe I didn't have as much closure with my husband's death as I had thought. But I really don't want to lose you. So . . . I guess I'm asking you if you could just be a little more patient?"

Jon thought for a moment. "Okay," he said. "But I *am* going to show you how much fun skating is."

"What are you talking about?" Susan asked, laughing.

"This," Jon said. He took her in his arms and kissed her.

Nearby, Max danced with Jill.

"So there was never any Marsh Monster?" Jill asked. "What did that kid see then?"

"It was just Deputy Potts coming from the bomb shelter," Max explained.

Jill's blue eyes sparkled at Max. "That is so awesome," she said. "I mean, you totally solved the crime on your own. You are so cool."

Max shrugged. "It was elementary."

Jill smiled at him. "You know, Max, in a couple years, you'll be older, and maybe . . . maybe you and I . . . could go out?"

Max paused for a moment, shocked. A week ago, he would have given up all his books for a chance to date Jill.

But that was a week ago. He had learned a lot since then. And just because someone was pretty on the outside, didn't always mean they were pretty on the inside.

"I don't think so," Max said carefully. "In a couple of years, we'll be different. Even more than we are now."

Max smiled. "But we'll always have French class!"

. . . ♥ . . .

Back at the Moody Mansion, Sauerkraut Slausen woke up from her nap. She took the cucumber slices off of her eyes and walked to the bathroom. Then she scrubbed off the cake icing.

Ms. Slausen looked in the mirror.

She gasped.

"It worked!" she cried.

Chapter Nineteen:
· · · Magic · · ·

The music from the celebration floated through the air as Roxy wandered through the grassy field. She looked at the stars twinkling in the sky.

"And so, the orphan Princess Roxahana finds herself once more alone," she said. "Will there be other adventures? Yes. But for now, she must be content with nothing but the stars above."

Roxy sighed dramatically. She started to walk back to the others.

Then she stopped.

Something glowed near the line of trees that ringed the park. It wasn't a flashlight. It was an unearthly glow, like nothing she'd ever seen.

The glowing light moved forward, and Roxy saw that it had a shape.

The shape of a little girl.

Sarah. The shaman's daughter.

Swiftfoot stood behind her, wagging his tail.

Sarah raised a ghostly hand and waved at Roxy. Roxy slowly raised her hand and waved back.

Then the glowing figure dissolved into the darkness . . .

"He was right," Roxy whispered. "It was magic."

Then Swiftfoot trotted toward Roxy. She opened her arms to greet him. He broke into a run, then jumped up into her arms.

"You know, Swiftfoot, in the words of the immortal Humpty Boogert, 'this looks like the start of a beautiful friendship,'" Roxy said.

Swiftfoot answered with a happy bark.